An Early I Can Read Book®

Silly Tilly
AND THE
Easter Bunny

story and pictures by

LILLIAN HOBAN

A Harper Trophy Book

Harper & Row, Publishers

Silly Tilly and the Easter Bunny
Copyright © 1987 by Lillian Hoban
All rights reserved. No part of this book may be
used or reproduced in any manner whatsoever without
written permission except in the case of brief quotations
embodied in critical articles and reviews. Printed in
the United States of America. For information address
Harper & Row Junior Books, 10 East 53rd Street,
New York, N.Y. 10022.

Library of Congress Cataloging-in-Publication Data
Hoban, Lillian.
    Silly Tilly and the Easter Bunny.

    (An Early I can read book)
    Summary: Silly Tilly Mole is so forgetful and silly
on Easter morning that she cannot find her bonnet and
nearly fails to let the Easter Bunny into the house.
    [1. Easter—Fiction.   2. Moles (Animals)—Fiction.
3. Rabbits—Fiction]   I. Title.   II. Series.
PZ7.H635Si   1987   [E]   86-7682
ISBN 0-06-022392-8
ISBN 0-06-022393-6 (lib. bdg.)

    (A Harper Trophy book)
ISBN 0-06-444127-X (pbk.)

First Harper Trophy edition, 1989.

To all grandmothers,
present and future

Silly Tilly Mole

woke up one morning.

She sniffed the wind.

"I smell jelly beans,"

she said.

She sniffed the wind again.

"It must be Easter,

and I forgot to remember."

Tilly heard a *thump*

on her front door.

"It is the Easter Bunny,"

she said.

"He is bringing me
my Easter basket.
I will ask him in
for a cup of tea.
First I will put on
my Easter bonnet."

Tilly reached for her glasses.

She could not find them.

"Oh dear," she said.

"I forgot to remember

where I put my glasses.

Don't go away, Mr. Bunny,"

she called.

8

Tilly looked under the bed.

She could not see

without her glasses,

and she forgot to remember

what she was looking for.

"I will light a candle,"
said silly Tilly.
"Then I will see
what I am looking for."
Tilly hurried downstairs
to get a candle.

10

But she could not see.

She bumped into a chair.

"Is that you, Mr. Bunny?"

she asked the chair.

"Do sit down.

I will make
a cup of tea for you
while I try to remember
what I am looking for."

13

Tilly scurried to the stove

to get the teapot.

But she forgot

where she was going.

14

She went
to the window
and got
a flowerpot
instead.

"Here is my Easter bonnet,"

she said.

She put the flowerpot

on her head.

"Thank goodness,"

said silly Tilly.

"I have found my Easter bonnet.

Now we can have our tea!"

She hurried to the table

to get the teacups.

17

"Oh, dear," said Tilly,

"I have hurried

so much

and scurried

so much,

I am in a tizzy.

I can't remember
why I am making tea.
And I forget
who it is for.
I must sit down
and think."

Just as Tilly sat down,

there was another loud *thump*

on her front door.

"My goodness!" she said.

"What a very loud *thump*!

I wonder who it could be?"

Tilly jumped up.

As she did,

her glasses slid

right onto her nose.

She could see!

"Oh, how nice!" she said.

"Here are my glasses!

Now I remember

what I was looking for.

Mr. Bunny," she called,

"are you still there?"

She hurried over to the chair.

"Oh, dear," she said.

"He isn't here.

He forgot to leave

my Easter basket,

and he didn't remember

his tea."

THUMP! THUMP! WHACK!

The front door flew open.

"Tilly Mole," called Mr. Bunny,

"I have brought

your Easter basket!"

"I thought

you forgot to remember,"

said Tilly.

"I would not forget,"

said the Easter Bunny.

"This is my job."

The Easter Bunny hopped

into the house.

"What a nice Easter bonnet,"

said Mr. Bunny.

"What a nice Easter basket,"

said Tilly Mole.

She could see

pink and purple jelly beans,

little candy Easter eggs,

a small chocolate bunny,

and a tiny yellow chick.

Tilly and the Easter Bunny

ate some jelly beans

with their tea.

And silly Tilly Mole said,

"I am so glad

you did not forget

to remember it is Easter!"